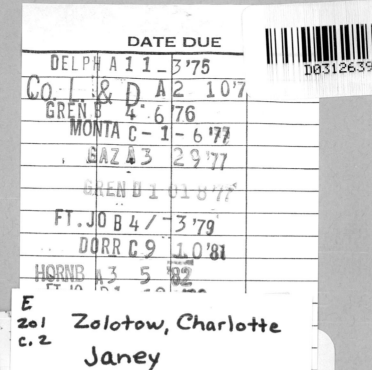

E
201
c.2

Zolotow, Charlotte

Janey

JANEY

by Charlotte Zolotow

Pictures by Ronald Himler

HARPER AND ROW, PUBLISHERS

New York, Evanston, San Francisco, London

JANEY

Text copyright © 1973 by Charlotte Zolotow
Illustrations copyright © 1973 by Ronald Himler

Library of Congress Catalog Card Number: 72–9861
Trade Standard Book Number: 06–026927–8
Harpercrest Standard Book Number: 06–026928–6

FIRST EDITION

To Stephie, Jenny, and Kerin

Janey
it's lonely
all day long
since you moved away.

When I walk in the rain
and the leaves are wet
and clinging to the sidewalk
I remember
how we used to walk
home·from school
together.

I remember how you had to touch
everything we passed,
the wet leaves
of the privet hedge,
even the stucco part
of the wall.
I only look with my eyes.

I still have the pebble
you found on the playground.
And I remember how
you skipped flat rocks
into the pond.
Mine just sank.

11

Sometimes when I'm playing
with the other kids
I remember how your voice sounded.
No one else sounds like you.

I remember sometimes
we both talked at once
and when we stopped
we'd said the same thing.
And I remember sitting on the steps
in the sun and not talking
at all.
There is no one else
I can sit with
and not talk.

I remember how
we'd go home for dinner
and I could hardly wait
for dinner to end
to call you.
But sometimes you called me first.

And I remember last Christmas
I half didn't want
to give you your present,
I wanted it so much myself.

You told me later
you half didn't want to give me mine
but when we each opened our present
it was the *same* book.
I think of you every time
I read the stories over again.

When the wind blows
through the trees at night
I remember how we used to
listen together
nights you slept over.

I didn't want you to move away.
You didn't want to either.
Janey
maybe some day
we'll grow up
and live near each other
again.

I wish you hadn't moved away.